Maybelle
in the
Soup

Katie Speck

Illustrations by Paul Rátz de Tagyos

SQUARE
FISH

Henry Holt and Company ◉ New York

For Erin, who laughed

—K. S.

SQUARE
FISH

An Imprint of Macmillan

Library of Congress Cataloging-in-Publication Data
Speck, Katie.
Maybelle in the soup / Katie Speck ; illustrations by Paul Rátz de Tagyos.
p. cm.
Summary: When Mr. and Mrs. Peabody invite guests to dinner, Maybelle, the cockroach who lives under their refrigerator, ignores the warnings of Henry the flea to be sensible and ends up "splashing" into a big adventure.
ISBN: 978-0-312-53598-8
[1. Cockroaches—Fiction. 2. Insects—Fiction. 3. Curiosity—Fiction.]
I. Rátz de Tagyos, Paul, ill. II. Title.
PZ7.S741185May 2007 [Fic]—dc22 2006033444

Originally published in the United States by Henry Holt and Company
Square Fish logo designed by Filomena Tuosto
Designed by Amelia May Anderson
First Square Fish Edition: 2009
10 9 8 7 6 5 4 3
www.squarefishbooks.com
LEXILE 760L

Contents

☙ 1 ☙

Bug Dreams

Maybelle was a lovely, plump cockroach. She lived with Myrtle and Herbert Peabody at Number 10 Grand Street, in her own cozy little home under the refrigerator.

The Peabodys liked everything to be JUST SO. "No dust, no mess, and absolutely, positively NO BUGS!" Mrs. Peabody was fond of saying.

Maybelle was not welcome, but she was a sensible cockroach. She obeyed The Rules: *When it's light, stay out of sight; if you're spied, better hide;* and, most important of all, *never meet with human feet.* The Peabodys didn't know they shared their kitchen with a bug.

Maybelle was sensible, but she *loved* food. And she wanted the good stuff. "I'm tired of crumbs and spills. I want tasty leftovers on a plate."

"Don't even think about it, kiddo," said her friend Henry the Flea. Henry lived and dined on the Peabodys' cat, Ramona. "If the Peabodys see you, they'll call the Bug Man. Then you'll be in a pickle."

"I might like a pickle, perhaps a pickle relish or pickled pigs' feet or—"

"We can't have exactly what we want," Henry said. "The Peabodys think dogs are messy, so I have to settle for a cat. Ramona bathes all day. I'm always wet. We've got to make the best of what we have, Maybelle."

Maybelle didn't think that making the best of what she had sounded very interesting. Just once she wanted to taste food before it hit the floor.

And that is how this story begins. Because a cockroach may not get exactly what a cockroach wants, but you can't blame her for trying.

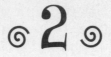

A Very Special Dinner

On Saturday, the Peabodys got ready for Very Important Guests. Mr. and Mrs. H. William Snodgrass were coming to dine. Everything had to be JUST SO.

Mr. Peabody set the dining room table with the best silver and china. Mrs. Peabody worked all day on a Very Special Dinner. The kitchen was full of wonderful smells.

Maybelle and Henry watched from under the refrigerator as Mrs. Peabody's dreadful big feet moved around the kitchen.

"Have you ever tasted a foot, Henry?" Maybelle thought about this sort of thing a lot.

"No way!" Henry said. "Humans may not notice a flea on their pets, but if a flea bites a foot, the Bug Man comes. I'll stick to my cat."

"I could sneak out for a little dinner before the guests arrive," Maybelle said. "I'd be very careful, Henry. I only want a teensy taste of the soup I smell. Mock turtle, Mrs. Peabody calls it."

"Mind your business, Maybelle," Henry said. "Stick to crumbs and spills."

Just then, Ramona's four furry feet appeared beside Mrs. Peabody's two big ones. "Well, there's *my* dinner," Henry said cheerfully, and off he hopped.

Maybelle sat by herself under the refrigerator and wondered, *What would it be like to eat mock turtle soup right out of a bowl?*

꩜ 3 ꩜

Soup's On

Ding-dong! At six o'clock the Peabodys'
Very Important Guests arrived.

The Peabodys were all dressed up to
greet them. Mr. Peabody was wearing a
few hairs carefully combed over his
shiny head. Mrs. Peabody was wearing
false eyelashes. They were long and
thick and made a little breeze when she
blinked. Both Peabodys were JUST SO.

Maybelle heard the H. William Snodgrasses exclaiming over the beautiful table in the dining room. She watched Mrs. Peabody's feet clomping in and out of the kitchen. She smelled the soup that sat in a bowl on the kitchen counter. And she wanted a taste.

When Mrs. Peabody went into the dining room with the salad, Maybelle couldn't be a sensible cockroach any longer. She broke the First Rule: *When it's light, stay out of sight.* She scurried out into the bright kitchen, then climbed onto the counter, crawled up the side of the china tureen, and looked down at the soup. She didn't see a turtle, but, oh, the beautiful brown broth and the lovely tomatoes and the—

At that very moment the kitchen door swung open. Mrs. Peabody hurried in. Maybelle was so startled that she lost her balance and teetered for a moment on the edge of the tureen. Then—*Plop! Splash!*—she fell into the soup!

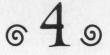

Maybelle in the Soup

Maybelle was going to be in terrible trouble if Mrs. Peabody saw her floating in the mock turtle soup. But then she remembered the Second Rule: *If you're spied, better hide.* She took a deep breath and went under.

Maybelle held her breath while Mrs. Peabody carried the big china tureen into the dining room. She held her breath while Mrs. Peabody put the tureen in the middle of the table. She held her breath while Mrs. Peabody ladled soup into four small bowls.

"This looks quite wonderful," Mrs. Snodgrass said, sniffing daintily at her bowl. "Everything in your home really is JUST SO."

"Why, of course it is." Mrs. Peabody smiled sweetly.

Maybelle held her breath while Mrs. Snodgrass picked up her spoon, dipped it into her soup, raised it to her lips and—

Maybelle couldn't hold her breath another instant. She stood up in the spoon with a gasp and found herself nose to nose with Mrs. Snodgrass!

With a yelp, Mrs. Snodgrass tossed
her spoon into the air. "*Eeeeee! Eeeeee!* A
bug in my soup! Oh, *disgusting*! I might
have *eaten* it!"

Maybelle sailed through the air and
landed on the butter dish. A nasty
human face had almost eaten her! She
began scrambling around the table in
a panic.

The room filled with squeals and
shouts. Humans swatted at Maybelle
with their napkins. The Peabodys' best

plates and glasses crashed to the floor.

"It's a roach!"

"Get it!"

"Smash the bug!"

Maybelle was so frightened that she fluttered from the tablecloth onto Mr. Peabody's shiny head. "Yuck!" Mr. Peabody cried and flicked her onto the front of Mrs. Snodgrass's dress.

"Yeeeee!" Mrs. Snodgrass screeched and swatted Maybelle high into the air. The humans yipped and hopped and overturned chairs in a rush to get out of the dining room before she landed.

When they were gone, the dining room was quiet. Maybelle found herself clinging to the chandelier and looking down on what was left of the Very Special Dinner.

❧ 5 ❧

A Bug on a Rug

Maybelle had never seen such a sight—
not tiny crumbs and dried spills, but
great globs of tasty leftovers. Nothing
was on a plate. Still, it was *almost*
exactly what she wanted!

Maybelle dropped from the chandelier to the rug and rushed about
trying everything—a chunk of blue
cheese on a slimy lettuce leaf, a gooey

lump of chopped goose liver, a smear of sweet butter with a shoe print in it.

Near the sideboard where Mrs. Peabody had put her special dessert, Maybelle found the best thing of all—whipped cream! One teeny taste and she forgot herself entirely. She plunged in all the way up to her second set of legs.

She couldn't see Ramona crouched over her. She couldn't hear Henry shout from the cat's right ear, "Look out, Maybelle!"

WHACK! Ramona's paw shot out and gave Maybelle a hard knock that sent her skidding across the rug. WHACK! Ramona sent her spinning in the other direction. Maybelle was so frightened that she could only flutter wildly. Ramona batted her one way and then the other.

"Run home! Run home!" Henry shouted.

With Ramona close behind, Maybelle ran as fast as her six legs could carry her. She scrambled across the dining room and through the kitchen. She fled to the safety of her home.

But she'd eaten too much. No matter how she struggled, she couldn't squeeze her belly through the narrow crack under the refrigerator.

Maybelle's desperate bottom stuck out into the kitchen. Ramona grabbed it and pulled.

Maybelle fainted.

๑ 6 ๑

A Surprise for
Mrs. Peabody

It was just as well that Maybelle didn't know where she was. Ramona carried the stunned bug in her sharp white teeth up the stairs and down the hall to the Peabodys' bedroom. A plump cockroach makes a fine gift.

In the bedroom, Mrs. Peabody was sitting up in bed with an ice pack on her head, weeping into a handkerchief.

"My lovely dinner party spoiled by a revolting cockroach!" she sobbed.

Mr. Peabody patted her arm. "Now, my dear. You mustn't upset yourself. Look who has come to cheer you up." Ramona stood proudly at the door with something in her mouth.

"Oh, Mama's angel! Mama's little comfort! Come to me, Precious!" Mrs. Peabody cried.

Ramona leaped up on the coverlet, put Maybelle down on her mistress's lap, and waited to hear what a very clever cat she was.

Meanwhile, Maybelle was waking from her faint. She lay on her back with her eyes squeezed shut and began gently

waving her legs in the air to see if she was dead.

Mrs. Peabody didn't have on her glasses. She leaned close to Maybelle. "What has my angel brought Mama?" She squinted and leaned closer, her nose almost touching Maybelle. Maybelle waved her legs—and Mrs. Peabody *saw*. She began to scream.

Maybelle and Ramona
both sailed through the air
as Mrs. Peabody leaped
from the bed.

"Roaches everywhere!
Do something, Herbert!" She clutched
her nightgown around her and
scrambled onto the top of
the dressing table.

Maybelle froze on the rug at
the foot of the bed, too frightened to
move. Mr. Peabody began throwing
things at her. Hairbrushes, pictures, and
books rained down.

"Oh for heaven's sake! Just step on
the thing, Herbert," Mrs. Peabody said
sternly from the dressing table.

Mr. Peabody lifted his big foot high over Maybelle. She'd broken the Third Rule. She was about to meet with human feet in a most unfortunate way. She was going to be squashed.

Instead she heard Mr. Peabody shout, "Ouch, I've been bitten! We have fleas, too!" He was so busy scratching his ankle that Maybelle had time to scramble under the bed.

"This will not do!" Mr. Peabody bellowed. "We'll call the Bug Man first thing in the morning."

❂ 7 ❂

Henry Hatches a Plan

"Hello, Bug Man!" Henry said, joining Maybelle under the bed.

Maybelle began to cry.

"On the other hand," said Henry, "that was pretty exciting. We've had an Adventure."

"Some adventure. The Bug Man will spray us," Maybelle howled.

Henry frowned and thought for a
moment. Then his tiny face cleared. "We
won't be here, kiddo. Problem solved."

"Where will we be?" Maybelle
sniffed.

"The Peabodys think bug spray is
smelly. They'll leave for a day or two
when the Bug Man comes. You hide in a
suitcase tonight. In the morning you'll be
off on a little vacation."

"What's a vacation?"

"Wait and see," Henry said.

"What about you?" Maybelle fretted.

"I'll be on vacation, too. Ramona goes where the Peabodys go. The Peabodys will go to a hotel. You'll like the hotel. They put chocolates on the pillows at night."

"Really? Chocolates on the pillows?" Maybelle cheered up. "You saved my life, Henry."

"Forget it," Henry said. "I've always wanted to bite a foot."

"How did it taste?" Maybelle was starting to feel hungry again.

"I would have preferred a golden retriever."

"Tell me more about the chocolates on the pillows," Maybelle said. The two friends talked late into the night, about chocolates and dogs and other tasty things.

The next morning Mrs. Peabody's suitcase was packed and ready by the front door. Arranged inside JUST SO were a skirt and blouse, a dressing gown, a makeup bag, and a pair of pink underpants with a lovely, plump cockroach hiding underneath.

꩜ 8 ꩜

Where's Henry?

Mrs. Peabody opened her suitcase in Room 1010 of the Grand Hotel. The Grand Hotel was even more JUST SO than the Peabodys' house—no dust, no mess, no bugs, and a sign in the lobby that said ABSOLUTELY, POSITIVELY NO GENTLEMEN WITHOUT COAT AND TIE. Maybelle and Henry were most definitely not welcome.

While the Peabodys unpacked, Maybelle crept under the bed to wait for Henry. Maybelle hadn't thought about anything but chocolate since the night before. Henry would tell her how to get it.

Maybelle waited and waited. While she waited, she listened to the voices of Mr. and Mrs. Peabody.

"I've had such a shock, Herbert," Mrs. Peabody whined. "My Very Special Dinner was ruined. And to think that there are nasty bugs in our house!"

"Not for long, my dear Myrtle. The Bug Man will take care of *that*. You can have another dinner party, a perfect one. In the meantime, we'll spend the evening right here at the Grand Hotel. We'll get just exactly what we want at the finest dining room in town. We'll forget all about bugs."

With that, the Peabodys left.

Maybelle sat alone in the dark under the bed. Was *this* the vacation that Henry had promised? Where was the chocolate? Where was Henry?

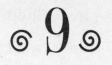

9

Under Wraps

"Hi there, kiddo!" Henry said, bounding cheerfully over the carpet.

"Henry! I thought you would never get here!"

"Sorry, Maybelle. I dozed off on Ramona. I like to nap after a good meal."

"Well, I haven't had a good meal since last night," Maybelle said, feeling grumpy. "When will the chocolate come?"

"Any time now, kiddo."

And while they watched from the darkness under the bed, a housekeeper bustled in. She smoothed the bedspread and turned down the sheets and placed a small piece of chocolate on each pillow. Then she left as quickly as she had come.

"Enjoy!" said Henry. "But watch out for Ramona."

Maybelle crept out from under the bed. There was no sign of the cat, so she climbed up the bedspread and peeked over the edge. There were chocolates on the pillows, all right. But *between* the pillows, Ramona was settled in for a catnap!

Ramona was a scary sight. But, oh, the lovely chocolates! Very slowly, Maybelle inched up the bedspread, hardly daring to breathe.

The cat snored softly as Maybelle reached the pillows. Then, with Maybelle a whisker's length away, Ramona twitched and stretched out a paw. Great hooked claws flashed in front of Maybelle's face! But the cat continued to snore.

When her heart stopped pounding, Maybelle threw herself on the chocolate. It smelled delicious. But there was something wrong—she couldn't taste it. It was wrapped!

"Wrapped!" she wailed once she was back under the bed with Henry. "You didn't tell me the chocolate was wrapped! What good is a hotel if you can't eat the chocolate?"

"I didn't know it would be wrapped," Henry said. "I never eat the stuff myself. But I'll make it up to you."

"How, Henry?" Maybelle was feeling sorry for herself.

"At hotels they have a thing called room service. Humans can stay right in their rooms and have meals brought up to them. When they're finished, they put their plates out in the hall. I've seen some things that would interest you on those plates, Maybelle."

"But won't it be dangerous in the hall? A human might see me. I might be *squashed!*"

"I'll come with you," Henry said. "I don't take chances at home, but we're on vacation. We're *supposed* to do things we wouldn't do at home. In fact," he added,

his legs beginning to twitch with excitement, "I saw a French poodle go into the next room. I've always wanted to try one of those!"

And so the two friends squeezed under the door of Room 1010 and into the hushed hallway of the Grand Hotel.

❧ 10 ❧

Maybelle on Wheels

Out in the hall, Maybelle saw what she'd always dreamed about—not crumbs and spills on the carpet but tasty leftovers on plates! *What a grand hotel!* Maybelle thought. She felt like a guest.

"I'm off to try some French food," Henry said. "See you back in our room before morning." And away he went to find his poodle, in great happy hops.

Maybelle hardly knew where to begin. There were plates up and down the hall. She wanted to nibble a bit from each one. Should she begin with the closest or the farthest? A cockroach on vacation has such lovely choices!

Maybelle was just about to make up her mind when she saw something that sent her heart racing: Two big shoes with a waiter in them were coming down the hall! The waiter was humming a little tune and piling all the plates on a cart.

Maybelle jumped into a green-bean casserole, and not a moment too soon. With a great clatter, the waiter picked up the plate where she hid and shoved it onto his cart. Then off he went.

Under the green beans, Maybelle wondered where she was going. How would she get back to Room 1010? Would she ever see her friend Henry again?

❧ 11 ❧

Eat and Be Eaten

The cart rolled and clattered along the hall, into the elevator, down to the first floor, and through a pair of swinging doors. They opened into the busiest room in the hotel—the kitchen.

This room was full of light and humans and feet. Humans tossed salads, stirred sauces, chopped vegetables, made bread. Everyone hurried.

And the noise! Spoons scraped, pots
banged, blenders whirred, and the sharp
blades of a garbage disposal roared in
the sink.

Maybelle wanted to stay hidden under her pile of green beans—she'd tasted worse—but someone was rinsing the food on the plates into the sink.

Maybelle felt a rush of fear. The terrible mouth of the garbage disposal opened wide. *A garbage disposal was going to eat her!*

When her dish was held under the faucet, she tried to hang on to it, but she was slippery with butter from the green beans. SWOOSH! Off she went down the drain.

The drain gushed with water that pushed Maybelle toward the disposal's great, grinding teeth. If only there was some way to climb out!

Suddenly, a long celery stalk washed into the drain and stood for a moment, half in, half out. Maybelle scrambled up the stalk as fast as she could and hung on. The stalk caught in the blades of the disposal and began to spin.

ZING! Maybelle shot across the kitchen and into a blender that whirred on the counter.

BOING! She bounced onto a twirling chunk of carrot. ZIP! She rocketed out of the blender, sailed through the air, and landed on a plate of food.

The kitchen workers were much too busy to notice Maybelle. Someone tucked parsley around her, clapped a silver lid over the plate, and sent it off to the dining room.

Safe in the dark under the lid, Maybelle was about to taste a hotel meal right off the plate in the finest dining room in town. This was more than even she had dared to want!

⊛ 12 ⊛

Hello Again!

Meanwhile, Mr. and Mrs. Peabody sat at a lovely table by the window, looking JUST SO. A waiter came their way, rolling a cart full of plates under silver lids. The Peabodys spread their napkins on their laps and prepared to be served.

With a flourish, the waiter took a plate from the cart and put it down in front of Mrs. Peabody. "For the lady," he said grandly, lifting the lid. "Breast of spring hen in a sauce of butter and garlic, topped with a—"

Maybelle sat on top of the hen with parsley tucked around her JUST SO. For one terrible moment, she and Mrs. Peabody looked at each other.

"COCKROACH!" Mrs. Peabody hollered and pushed away from the table so hard that her chair tipped over. She landed on her back with her legs sticking straight up in the air.

"I beg your pardon, madam," the waiter said with great dignity, addressing her shoes.

"Cockroach!" she whimpered from the floor.

"Surely not, madam. There are no bugs at the Grand Hotel."

"If my wife says that she saw a cockroach, she saw a cockroach!" Mr. Peabody growled, helping his wife to her feet. "And at these prices!"

In all the excitement, Maybelle fled to Mrs. Peabody's purse, the nearest dark place she could find. She comforted herself by sucking on a breath mint. Two human faces in two days!

Mrs. Peabody picked up her purse and let Mr. Peabody help her out of the dining room. "Bugs! Horrible bugs!" they muttered as they went.

Behind them, a room full of nervous diners scratched their ankles and checked under their lettuce leaves for insects.

Maybelle spent the rest of the night waiting for Henry in Room 1010. Henry didn't come.

✇ 13 ✇

Checkout

In the morning, the Peabodys packed their bags. Maybelle went with them to the lobby, still in Mrs. Peabody's purse. She couldn't bear going back to Number 10 Grand Street without Henry. Where was he? Not on Ramona—the cat hadn't scratched herself all night.

While Maybelle worried over Henry, Mr. Peabody gave the hotel manager a piece of his mind. "Grand Hotel indeed! There are bugs in this hotel. Your waiter served my wife a cockroach in the dining room last night!" Mr. Peabody fumed.

"Impossible!" exclaimed the manager, turning red in the face.

"Not at all," said a woman holding a little white poodle. "Our precious Poopsie scratched all night. This hotel has fleas, too. Poor Poopsie is going to get a flea dip at once!"

Suddenly Maybelle remembered something Henry had said about napping after a good meal. He was asleep on the poodle. Henry was going to get a flea dip! And it was Maybelle's fault, for

not obeying The Rules or sticking with
crumbs and spills.

Maybelle had to wake Henry, but
she'd have to break all The Rules at once
to do it. She dropped from the darkness
of the purse to the floor and scurried in
plain sight through a forest of human feet.

"Ack!" said Poopsie's owner, pointing
at Maybelle.

"There's *another* bug!" screeched Mrs. Peabody.

"A cockroach!" roared Mr. Peabody, stamping his foot at Maybelle and missing her by an antenna.

"I'll handle this, sir!" The manager stamped both feet, one–two, one–two. Maybelle had to zigzag wildly to avoid being squashed.

Ramona was curled in Mr. Peabody's arms, her eyes wide with fear. When Maybelle scrambled up the inside of Mr. Peabody's pant leg, his eyes got wide, too, and he began jigging and shaking his leg and making odd sounds.

With a loud hiss, Ramona jumped to the floor and ran across the lobby. Poopsie the poodle went yapping after her.

"Stop, Poopsie!" her owner cried.

But Poopsie and Ramona rolled together in a yelping, spitting ball of flying fur.

Mr. Peabody reached into the fur ball and pulled Ramona out. "We came to this hotel to get away from bugs and what do we get?" he bellowed. "More bugs—and vicious dogs, too! Shame!"

The hotel manager's face was even redder than before. Off he went to call the Bug Man.

In all the confusion, Maybelle fell out of Mr. Peabody's pants and crawled back into the purse Mrs. Peabody had dropped on the floor. Now she peeked out at Ramona and waited hopefully. Sure enough, Ramona began to scratch. Henry would be going home with Maybelle after all!

The Peabodys left the lobby with their cat, their suitcases, their noses in the air, and the only two bugs in the Grand Hotel.

໑ 14 ໑

Home Sweet Home

Back at Number 10 Grand Street, the Peabodys turned off the kitchen light on their way to bed.

"It's good to be home, isn't it, dear?" Mr. Peabody said.

"Yes, Herbert. It's good to be out of that awful hotel. Everything here is JUST SO again—no dust, no mess, and absolutely, positively NO BUGS!" With

a deep sigh of contentment, Mrs. Peabody followed her husband up the stairs.

In the dark kitchen, the refrigerator whirred softly. Safe and cozy in Maybelle's home, Maybelle and Henry talked about their vacation.

"The best part of a vacation is coming home, if you ask me," Maybelle said.

Henry smiled. "The poodle was nice."

"The breast of spring hen with butter and garlic was nice, too," Maybelle admitted. "But from now on I'll make the best of what I have. Crumbs and spills aren't really so bad. Anyway, we can't have exactly what we want." Maybelle said this as if she'd thought of it herself. "No more adventures, Henry."

"Suits me, kiddo."

"Of course," Maybelle said, "I might like a nice jelly omelet, or maybe a chocolate pudding with green peas and carrots on top. That would look nice in a blue bowl, don't you think, Henry? Or maybe…"

Well, even if a cockroach can't get exactly what a cockroach wants, you can't blame her for dreaming.

FLIP ME OVER
to read another great story about Maybelle!

Maybelle
Goes to Tea

Katie Speck

Illustrations by Paul Rátz de Tagyos

SQUARE
FISH

Henry Holt and Company ☉ New York

For Allen, my first reader and best friend

—K. S.

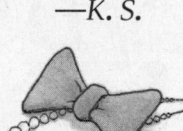

SQUARE
FISH

An Imprint of Macmillan

MAYBELLE GOES TO TEA. Text copyright © 2008 by Katie Speck. Illustrations
copyright © 2008 by Paul Rátz de Tagyos. All rights reserved. Printed in March 2010
in the United States of America by R. R. Donnelley & Sons Company,
Harrisonburg, Virginia. For information, address Square Fish,
175 Fifth Avenue, New York, NY 10010.

Square Fish and the Square Fish logo are trademarks of Macmillan and
are used by Henry Holt and Company under license from Macmillan.

Library of Congress Cataloging-in-Publication Data
Speck, Katie.
Maybelle goes to tea / Katie Speck ; illustrations by Paul Rátz de Tagyos.
p.   cm.
Summary: Maybelle the cockroach follows the advice of her new fly
friend Maurice and tumbles into a terrifying but tasty adventure during
Mrs. Peabody's Ladies' Spring Tea.
ISBN: 978-0-312-53598-8
[1. Cockroaches—Fiction. 2. Insects—Fiction. 3. Afternoon teas—Fiction.]
I. Rátz de Tagyos, Paul, ill. II. Title.
PZ7.S741185Mag 2008   [Fic]—dc22   2007040937

Originally published in the United States by Henry Holt and Company
Square Fish logo designed by Filomena Tuosto
First Square Fish Edition: 2009
10 9 8 7 6 5 4 3
www.squarefishbooks.com

LEXILE 550L

Contents

❂ 1 ❂

Red Hot!

Myrtle and Herbert Peabody were quite sure there were ABSOLUTELY, POSITIVELY NO BUGS in their house at Number 10 Grand Street. That's because Maybelle the Cockroach behaved herself. She obeyed all three of The Rules: *When it's light, stay out of sight; if you're spied, better hide;* and *never meet with human feet.*

But there are Cockroach Cautions, too. One night Maybelle ignored a very important one: *Test before you taste.* She found a tiny red spill on the kitchen floor, and she loved food *so* much and got *so* excited that she forgot about the cautions altogether. Nobody's perfect.

"Raspberry jam!" she said to herself. "My favorite thing, after chocolate."

She didn't use her antennae to sniff the spill, and she didn't take a weensy taste. She didn't *test* at all. She dove right in, face first.

She got an unpleasant surprise. It was *not* raspberry jam. It was red-hot pepper sauce. It was *so* hot that she jigged and

danced around the floor. She felt as if she'd eaten a fire ant.

"OH! OUCH!"

Maybelle dashed for the sink and hung upside down off the end of the faucet. She needed a drop of water to cool her mouth parts. But she waited . . . and waited . . . and waited. The faucet didn't leak. Everything was JUST SO at Number 10 Grand Street.

"What are you doing, kiddo?" Henry the Flea said when he hopped by for a visit.

"I'm waiting," Maybelle grumbled. "I'm waiting for this faucet to leak. I'm 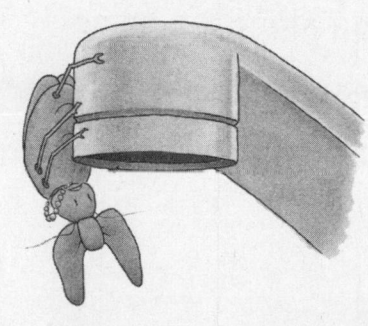 waiting for my mouth to stop burning. I'm waiting for something *delicious.*"

"I'm waiting for a golden retriever," Henry said. "But I've got a cat. You've got crumbs and spills. We make the best of what we have, remember?"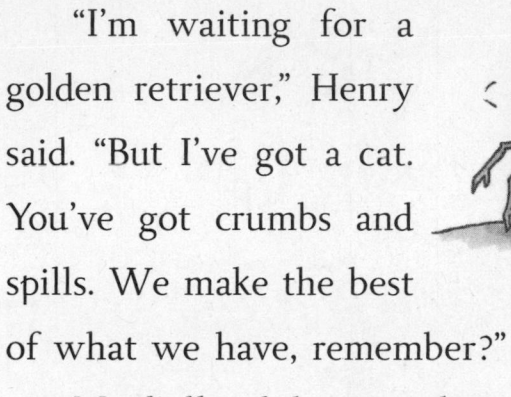

Maybelle did remember. And she knew that adventures happen to a cockroach who breaks The Rules. She would try to be content eating crumbs and spills in the dark, like any other cockroach. She didn't want an adventure.

But adventure was about to come along anyway. Because whether a cockroach is behaving herself or she isn't, life is full of surprises.

⟲ 2 ⟲

Belly Up

The next morning, Maybelle and Henry watched from Maybelle's home under the refrigerator as the Peabodys hurried out the kitchen door. They were off to buy goodies for Mrs. Peabody's Ladies' Spring Tea. It was an Extra Special occasion. Only the Best People were invited.

But when the Peabodys went out, someone zoomed in without an invitation.

"BRZZZT! Maurice here!" said a very large fly. "Coming in."

As soon as he was in, Maurice began trying to get out. "BRZZZT! Going out."

He wasn't going out. The Peabodys were gone, the door was closed, and a big, noisy fly was trapped in the kitchen.

"Going out! Going out!" Maurice said, throwing himself against the door.

"Going out!" he said, crashing into the wall.

"This is going to be trouble," Henry said to Maybelle.

"What will we do?" Maybelle said to Henry.

"BRZZZZZT! Going out!" Maurice cried. And he smacked up against the windowpane so hard that he knocked himself insensible.

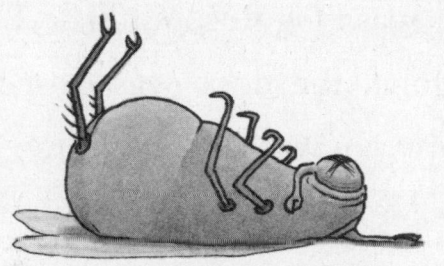

Maurice lay on the windowsill with his legs in the air for what seemed a very long time. Even belly-up, he was Noticeable. And Unwelcome. And likely to cause an Extermination Event at Number 10 Grand Street.

"Come on, Maybelle. We've got to hide him before the Peabodys see him and call the Bug Man," Henry said.

"I'm not going out there. What if Ramona the Cat catches me?"

"Don't worry. Ramona is busy bird-watching in an upstairs window."

Maybelle *was* worried, but she didn't want a visit from the Bug Man. So the two friends ventured out into the kitchen.

When it's light, stay out of sight! The day had hardly begun, and Maybelle had already broken The First Cockroach Rule.

⚙ 3 ⚙

Carry On

With Henry bouncing along beside her,
Maybelle scuttled across the floor and
up the wall to the windowsill where
Maurice lay.

Maybelle didn't like the look of him.
He had bug eyes, hairy legs, and his feet
smelled like sour milk. Still, there was
nothing to do but get him on her back
and carry him home.

Maybelle made herself as flat as she could. "Get under him and push, Henry."

Henry hopped, and panted, and shoved against the big fly. Finally, with a desperate heave, he managed to load Maurice onto Maybelle's back. "To the refrigerator!" he cried.

But before Maybelle had gotten even halfway there, the Peabodys returned. Luckily, they could hardly see over their bulging grocery bags.

"Even Mildred Snodgrass is coming to my Ladies' Spring Tea," Mrs. Peabody said as she struggled into the kitchen. "It will be the social event of the year, Herbert. It must be Extra Special."

"I'm sure it will be perfection, Myrtle," Herbert Peabody said.

Maybelle scrambled frantically among

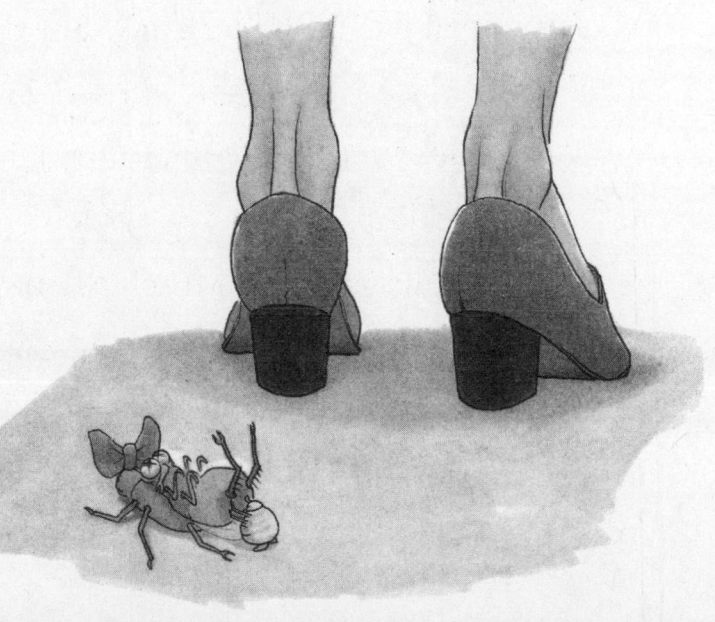

12

human feet, darting this way and that. She had to get home as fast as possible. The Peabodys would see her when they put their bags down. If they saw her, the Bug Man would come. If they *stepped* on her . . .

"Hurry!" Henry shouted.

Maybelle hurried so fast that Maurice nearly slid off her back. But she made it to the refrigerator, stuffed him into the crack that was her front door, and followed him in.

"There!" she said. "We'll tell Maurice how things are done around here when he wakes up."

"If you say so, kiddo." Henry sounded doubtful.

⚬ 4 ⚬

Go for It!

Maybelle and Henry watched Mrs. Peabody from Maybelle's door. First she took a teapot with matching cups and saucers from the cupboard. Then she piled platters high with tea cakes, biscuits, and sandwiches with the crusts cut off. And just before she went upstairs to dress for the party, she arranged Chocolate Surprise Cookies on her best plate.

"I wonder what the surprise *is*, Henry. Don't you?"

"Maybe there'll be crumbs on the floor tonight and you can find out."

"I want to taste the surprise while it's still in the cookie," Maybelle said.

"We're making the best of what we have. Remember, kiddo?"

Maybelle remembered. And she wasn't happy about it.

While the two friends talked, Maurice recovered from his crash. He tested his wings. "BZZZRT! Any garbage in here?"

"Certainly not! This is Number 10 Grand Street. Everything here is JUST SO," Maybelle said.

"Yeah, right, right. So what *do* you have to eat, huh?" Maurice rubbed his legs together vigorously. "Any rotten eggs? Moldy cheese? How about some spoiled meat? BZRRRT!" He rubbed his legs faster and faster.

Before Maybelle could answer, he saw the Ladies' Spring Tea spread out on the kitchen counter. Everything was arranged on the plates JUST SO.

"Never mind, Missy. Gonna get me some *goodies!*"

"You can't do that!" Maybelle cried. "There are Rules here. If we don't obey them, the Bug Man comes."

"BRZZZT! I've got my own Rule, Missy," Maurice said. *"Go for it!"*

And he did.

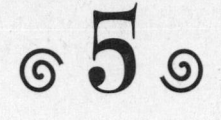

Cockroach Sandwich

"I don't like Maurice," Maybelle said to Henry. "He's very irritating. He's noisy. He rubs his hairy legs together. His feet smell. And he calls me Missy."

"Don't be too hard on him, Maybelle," Henry said. "You never know. Sometimes when you think you couldn't like someone at all, they surprise you."

Maybelle peeked out to see what Maurice was up to. What she didn't like the *most* about him was that he was getting to eat all the delicious treats *she* wanted. He was buzzing and rubbing and treading all over everything with his smelly feet. When he landed on the Chocolate Surprises, Maybelle had had enough.

"This won't do, Henry! Rules or no Rules, I'm going out there!"

Maybelle didn't know that Ramona was no longer bird-watching upstairs— she was crouched in front of the refrigerator. Maybelle barged out of her cozy little home right under the cat's nose.

Ramona's eyes were wide with excitement. *WHAM!* She reached out a paw and whacked Maybelle hard on her bottom. *WHAM!* She whacked her again. It was too late for the terrified cockroach to turn back—the cat blocked her way. So Maybelle bolted forward instead and headed for the counter. Ramona was barely a whisker's length behind her.

"GO! GO!" Henry said.

"BZRRRT!" Maurice stood on the ceiling, watching the chase and rubbing his legs together.

Maybelle jumped on the first plate she came to. She wriggled in between a slice of cucumber and a piece of buttered bread and held her breath.

Ramona swatted at Maybelle's sandwich. "Raaoow!"

"No, Precious!" Mrs. Peabody said, hurrying into the kitchen. "There's nothing in that cucumber sandwich that a kitty would like. It's for the ladies."

Mrs. Peabody put Ramona on the floor, gave her a pat, and took the sandwiches and the other goodies into the parlor.

Maybelle went to her very first Ladies' Spring Tea.

⚙ 6 ⚙

Teatime

The ladies looked grand. They were powdered and polished and dressed in their best clothes. Mrs. Snodgrass even wore a new hat with decorations piled on top that looked like shiny little fruits—apples and oranges and lemons.

"Why, Myrtle, everything on the tea table is Just So. What lovely treats!" she said.

Maurice agreed. He invited himself to the party and zoomed among the ladies. "BRZZZT!"

Maybelle peeked out of her cucumber sandwich. "Oh, dear," she said to no one in particular.

"Shoo!" Mrs. Peabody cried, flapping her hand at Maurice.

All the ladies joined in, shooing and flapping. Ramona tried to help, too. But Maurice paid them no mind. He was going for it.

Mrs. Peabody's face turned red with embarrassment. She called Mr. Peabody in from the yard. "You must do something, Herbert! Get the fly swatter."

"Let me handle this, ladies," he announced. He began stalking Maurice, fly swatter upraised.

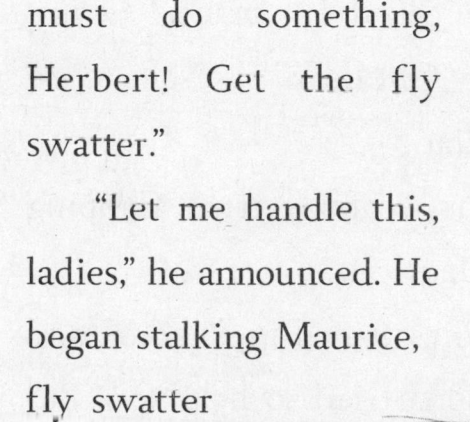

Maurice landed on the biscuits. *BAM!*
Mr. Peabody smashed the biscuits but

missed Maurice. Maurice landed on the
tea cakes. *BAM!* Mr. Peabody crushed
the tea cakes, but Maurice was already
on the cucumber sandwiches.

"Over there!" the ladies urged. Mr.
Peabody was excited by the chase.

Maurice was everywhere at once. *SMACK! SMACK!* When he alighted on Mrs. Snodgrass's hat—*BAM!*—little fruits flew into the air. They hit the floor and bounced and rolled like marbles.

There was a moment of shocked silence. "You've ruined my new hat. I didn't come here to be attacked by filthy insects," Mrs. Snodgrass snapped.

"Anyone could have a fly in the house," Sue Ellen Snerdly said.

Then another of the ladies pointed at a plate. "*That's* a cockroach!"

Maybelle sat stunned and exposed on what was left of the cucumber sandwiches. She wore a piece of buttered bread on her head.

If you're spied, better hide! Maybelle skittered for cover under the carpet. At the sight of a skittering cockroach, the ladies panicked and fled across the little

fruits from Mrs. Snodgrass's hat. The
fruits rolled, and the ladies slid and
slipped and sprawled and crawled to get
out of the house.

Mrs. Snerdly regained her feet at the
door, straightened her dress, and smiled.
"Thank you for the tea party. It was
Extra Special. It isn't *so* terrible to have
a cockroach in the cucumber sandwiches."

Mrs. Peabody began to sob. Her
Ladies' Spring Tea was over.

⊚ 7 ⊚

In a Fog

The only things that managed to survive Mr. Peabody's fly swatter were the Chocolate Surprises and the fly. Maurice buzzed around and enjoyed what was left of the party.

Mrs. Peabody wiped her eyes and blew her nose. "I'm feeling faint, Herbert," she announced.

"Put your head down and breathe, dear. *Breathe!*" Mr. Peabody said.

"My tea party is ruined!" Mrs. Peabody sniffed from between her knees. "Call the Bug Man, Herbert!"

"No need, dear, I'll handle this myself. I'm going to set off a Bug Bomb. We'll wait in the yard. And in a little

while there will be absolutely, positively NO BUGS at Number 10 Grand Street."

Mr. Peabody helped Mrs. Peabody outside. He carried Ramona. Mrs. Peabody carried the plate of Chocolate Surprises. "You know I eat when I'm upset, Herbert," she sniffed.

"A little fresh air will do you a world of good, Myrtle."

Mr. Peabody closed all the windows and put a Bug Bomb in the parlor. He pushed the button on the bomb and rushed out into the yard.

One, two, three—the Bug Bomb sent a deadly fog drifting through the house.

Under the carpet, Maybelle's heart raced. "We've got to get out of here, Henry!"

"We can go through Ramona's cat door. But we have to go *now*," Henry said. The white fog was spreading across the parlor, coming closer and closer. "Follow us, Maurice."

Maurice had difficulty taking directions. "BRZZZZT! Going out." He threw himself against the wall. "Going out!" He threw himself against the door. "Going out, going out!" He threw himself against the window with a great *THWACK!* Maurice lay belly-up on the windowsill.

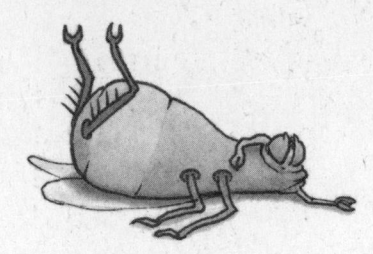

"Not again," Maybelle moaned. "Now what?"

But she knew what had to be done. The poisonous fog drifted their way. There was no time to spare. Little Henry grunted and strained and loaded the fly onto Maybelle's back.

Maybelle didn't care for Maurice, but he was a bug. Bugs stick together— even if one of them is very irritating.

8

Go for It?

Maybelle and Henry shoved Maurice through the cat door and found themselves in Mr. Peabody's yard.

The outside of Number 10 Grand Street was every bit as JUST SO as the inside. Mr. Peabody kept the grass cut to *exactly* two inches. He clipped all the shrubs into neat balls. And he put a sign on the lawn that said "STAY OFF THE

GRASS: ABSOLUTELY, POSITIVELY NO CHILDREN OR DOGS!" Maybelle thought it might be wise to hide. She and Henry left Maurice on the stoop and crawled under the doormat.

From their hiding place, the two friends watched the Peabodys. The humans sat side by side on lawn chairs with the plate of Chocolate Surprises close at hand.

"Mrs. Snodgrass will never forgive us!" Mrs. Peabody said. "I'm very upset, Herbert." She popped a Surprise into her mouth. "I don't know when I've been so upset." She popped another Surprise into her mouth.

Maybelle looked at the plate of Surprises. Surely, Mrs. Peabody couldn't eat any more. There was only one left now. Maybelle had wondered all morning what the surprise *was*. She might never know. Unless...

"I'm going to find out what's in that cookie," Maybelle said.

"You can't do that, kiddo. That would be *really* dangerous. Stay here until it's safe to go back in the house. As for me"—

Henry eyed Ramona, who was settling down for a nap in the sun—"I'm going to get a hot lunch." And he bounded off to his cat.

"Everyone else has something good to eat," Maybelle thought out loud. "I've been in danger all day and I have nothing to show for it. Maybe Maurice has the right idea."

So Maybelle took a deep breath, counted "One, two, three," and rushed out from under the doormat. *"Go for it!"* she cried and made a run at the last cookie.

❂ 9 ❂

Foolish Pleasure

The Peabodys were looking in the other direction. They didn't see Maybelle coming. But Ramona did. She woke up and scratched at the flea behind her ear just as Maybelle charged by.

"Uh-oh. Look out, Maybelle!" Henry shouted. His hot lunch leaped up and began the chase.

With Ramona in pursuit, Maybelle ran until she reached the cookie. And with no time to sniff or taste or test, she plunged into the mysterious heart of the last Chocolate Surprise.

Soft, creamy fudge—that's what she found inside. It wasn't especially surprising. But it was so delicious that she forgot Rules and Cautions and humans and cats.

BOP!

Ramona didn't forget about a certain plump cockroach. *BAT!* She reached out and batted the cookie. Then she batted it some more. *BAT! BAT!*

"Oh my, Herbert. Look at silly Ramona!" Myrtle Peabody said. "She wants my cookie. No, naughty kitty, it's for Mommy. Cookies *comfort* Mommy."

And with that, Mrs. Peabody stuffed the Surprise into her mouth. If she'd bothered to look at it first, she might have noticed that it had legs and a bottom.

⑩ 10 ⑨

A Chocolate Surprise

Inside the cookie, Maybelle was immersed in heavenly fudge. It was worth every minute of the danger she'd faced that day—until she noticed that something was very wrong. Her cookie was getting warm and wet. She began to struggle.

"BLECK!" Mrs. Peabody cried at the same moment. "BLECK! BLECK!"

"Whatever is the matter, dear?" Mr. Peabody said.

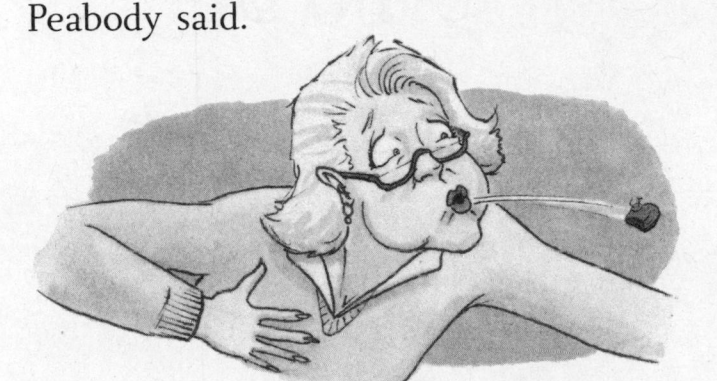

"BLECK!" Mrs. Peabody leaped out of her chair and spit the Chocolate Surprise out on the grass. "ICK! ICK! ICK! There's a bug in that cookie! Oh, *bleck!* I'm going to faint, Herbert."

Mr. Peabody leaped up and helped her back into her chair. "Put your head between your knees, dear, and breathe. *Breathe!*"

"But it *moved*, Herbert. I felt its nasty legs!"

"Breathe, dear. I'll handle this." Mr. Peabody stood over the mushy glob of Chocolate Surprise and raised his foot.

Never meet with human feet! It was too late—Maybelle had broken the Third Rule.

Then Mr. Peabody looked at his clean shiny shoe. It wouldn't be JUST SO if he used it to smash a cookie with a bug in it. So he went off to get a more suitable weapon. He came back with a shovel.

"What are you going to do, Herbert?"

"I'm going to scoop up the cookie and throw it over the fence into the

neighbor's yard. They won't care about the mess and the bug. They have children and a dog."

So Maybelle sailed over the fence in a wet Surprise and landed at Number 8 Grand Street.

❦ 11 ❦

As the Crow Flies

Maybelle squirmed out of the cookie. She was unchewed but very frightened. And she'd had quite enough Surprise for one day. Now she wanted to go home. She was wondering exactly where home was when a shadow fell across her.

Maybelle looked up a long beak into the beady black eyes of a crow. PECK! PECK! Somebody *else* was trying to eat

her. She scrambled away, but the bird followed. PECK! HOP! PECK! The faster Maybelle ran, the faster the crow hopped.

Suddenly—HOP, PECK, WHOOSH!—Maybelle was in its beak and soaring into the sky. She squeezed her eyes shut.

When she opened them again, the crow was circling the tree in the back-yard of Number 10 Grand Street. In a branch below, Maybelle saw a nest full of baby birds with very big mouths. "*Peep, peep!* Me first!" they all cried at once. The mother crow was about to feed Maybelle to a lucky nestling.

Suddenly, "BRZZT! BRZZT! BRZZZT!" Maurice was everywhere at once. He buzzed around the crow's eyes. He

dashed. He dove. He buzzed some more.
He was very, very irritating. The crow
shook its head to shoo him off, but
Maurice paid no attention.

"BRZZZZT! Drop her, girlie!" he
cried. "BRZZZT!" He was *so* irritating that
the crow opened its mouth to protest.

And Maybelle was falling, falling....

☙ 12 ☙

Another Belly, Up

Mrs. Peabody sat slumped in her lawn chair while Mr. Peabody fanned her face. "You've had a horrible experience, Myrtle. But I've taken care of the problem. Try to relax and enjoy the outdoors. There are now absolutely, positively NO BUGS in the yard at Number 10 Grand Street."

Mrs. Peabody had no time to reply. Maybelle landed on her head. *Plop!*

At almost the same moment, "CAW! CAW!" The crow flapped down to snatch Maybelle for her babies. And...

Maurice zoomed around the crow's head to protect Maybelle. "BRZZZT! Scram, birdie!" And...

Ramona saw a cockroach, a bird, and a fly in her mistress's hair, all at once. She crouched. Henry tried to distract the cat by biting her, but she was too excited to notice. "RAUOOOW!" She leaped onto Mrs. Peabody's head.

"EEEEH!" Mrs. Peabody screeched. She jumped up, slapping and swatting at herself. "AWWWK! Falling bugs! Vicious birds! Even Ramona has attacked me! I want to go back inside."

Everyone scattered. The crow flew back to her tree. Maurice zoomed away. Ramona fled across the yard. And Maybelle, for lack of a better idea, hid under Mrs. Peabody's chair.

"I'm going to faint, Herbert," Mrs. Peabody said. But this time she knew just what to do about it. She breathed, and she put her head between her knees. She and Maybelle found themselves looking at each other nose to nose.

Without another word, Mrs. Peabody *did* faint. She somersaulted out of her chair and sprawled belly-up on the grass.

Mr. Peabody was so surprised, he didn't notice Maybelle. "Oh dear!" he said. He fanned his wife's face and patted her cheeks, but she remained insensible. So Mr. Peabody gently loaded Mrs. Peabody into his wheelbarrow and rolled her into the house.

It was safe now. The Bug Bomb had done its work. There were ABSOLUTELY, POSITIVELY NO BUGS at Number 10 Grand Street. Yet.

Maybelle had had quite enough of the outdoors. She wanted to go back inside, too. Henry joined her for the journey home. He kept an eye out for Ramona and the crow while Maybelle talked.

"I'm going to behave from now on," she said. "I'm going to obey The Rules. *Go for it* is not the best idea for a cock-roach. It causes adventures."

At the house, Maybelle scurried across the mat and through the cat door into the kitchen.

The mat said "WELCOME!"

⚙ 13 ⚙

Red Hot? Not!

The next day, Mrs. Peabody baked a pie.

"I've made my Extra Special Raspberry Rapture as a surprise for Mrs. Snodgrass, Herbert. I know she'll forgive us for ruining her hat when she tastes the pie. It is JUST SO."

"I'm sure it's perfection, dearest. I'll take you out to lunch to celebrate," Mr. Peabody said.

Before they left, Mrs. Peabody opened the kitchen window, closed the screen, and put the pie on the sill to cool. There was no need to cover it. There were no bugs in the house.

Maybelle looked at the pie from her safe little home under the refrigerator. Ripe red raspberries were her favorite thing, after chocolate. And here was a whole pie with a lovely brown crust.

"Where is Ramona?" Maybelle asked Henry.

"She's outside under the tree staring at the crow's nest."

"Well, in that case," said Maybelle, "I'm going to have a taste of the Raspberry Rapture Pie."

Henry didn't point out that Maybelle had promised to obey The Rules only the day before. After all, he thought, nobody's perfect.

Maybelle walked around on the pie. She sniffed and tasted and tested. Then she settled down in the center and began to eat. The pie *was* perfection.

"I like Maurice," she said between bites. "He was nice, wasn't he? I mean, except for his eyes and his feet and his hairy legs and some other things. It's awfully quiet around here without him."

"Just like I said, kiddo. Sometimes, when you think you couldn't like someone at all, they surprise you."

"BZZZRT!" *WHAM!* Maurice hit the window screen. "Hey, Missy!" He rubbed his legs together. "Got anything rotten in there?"

Maybelle was happy to see him. "Certainly not," she said, "but you could come in the cat door and share this pie with me."

"No, thanks. Better stuff across the fence—moldy peanut butter sandwiches, rotten banana peels, dog p—"

"Ssssh! There's a lady present," said Henry.

"Oh, right, right! Gotta go. Kid at Number 8 just dropped an ice cream cone. Gotta get to it before the ants do. BRZZZZT!" Maurice was gone.

"I think I'll go next door for a bite, too," Henry said. "That dog over there could be a golden retriever. You never know."

Maybelle ate Mrs. Snodgrass's Extra Special Raspberry Rapture Pie and thought about life. Henry was right. You never know. She certainly never expected

to have a noisy, irritating friend with bug eyes, hairy legs, and smelly feet. But she did. And she might even learn to like being called Missy. Missy Maybelle.

She rubbed her front legs together and had another bite of pie.

One thing is for sure, she decided. Whether you're behaving yourself or you're not, life is full of surprises.

FLIP ME OVER

to read another great story about maybelle!